ZACK AND IKE
ARE EXACTLY
ALIKE

SUZANNE BLOOM

ASTRA YOUNG READERS

AN IMPRINT OF ASTRA BOOKS FOR YOUNG READERS

New York

Zack and Ike
are exactly alike.

wriggly hair

googly glasses

giggly grins

strong muscles

kind hearts

stripy shirts

helmets

Ike has a backpack just like Zack.

Zack has a bike just like Ike.

Every day they race downhill through the sea serpent's swamp to their secret hideout.

They unpack their tools
and get to work.

Or they explore

or practice tricks

or wrassle

or read.

"Let's go for a hike," said Ike.

"Let's go back," said Zack.

"Look. Tracks," said Zack.
"Our hideout was attacked!"

"Yikes!" said Ike.

"Must be a monster.
Stand back, Zack."

"I'm not
scared."

"Ooooooh.
It's a puppy."
It was snoring.

"Let's call him Spike," said Ike.
"Let's call him Mack," said Zack.

After a snack

they practiced new tricks.

And they read for a while.
Zack and Ike liked being exactly alike.

Then along came
Zena Lola-Jo Lee,

and she was exactly different.

Or was she?

To my Merryweathers—
Rebecca D. and Barbara G.
—SB

For information about permission to reproduce selections from this book,
please contact permissions@astrapublishinghouse.com.

Astra Young Readers
An imprint of Astra Books for Young Readers, a division of Astra Publishing House
astrapublishinghouse.com

Printed in China

ISBN: 978-1-63592-572-2 (hc)
ISBN: 978-1-63592-573-9 (eBook)
Library of Congress Control Number: 2021906405

First edition
10 9 8 7 6 5 4 3 2 1

Design by Barbara Grzeslo
The text is set in Neutraface.
The illustrations are done in gouache and colored pencil.